GET REAL, MALLORY!

Daisy Hirst

WALKER BOOKS
AND SUBSIDIARIES

LONDON • BOSTON • SYDNEY • AUCKLAND

I am not really the best at
drawing dogs.

But I showed Dad and he said,
"He's got a great smile, Nomi,
so friendly!"

So I called him Mallory and
put stars around him.

Stephen said, "Nomi, can you move?
I have so much homework. I have more
homework than anyone ever.
It will never, ever be done."

"I could help!" I said.

"Ha!" said Stephen.
"Get real, Nomi! And why is
your bear in the sky?"

"It's a dog," I said.

He said, "You're
better at drawing fish."

"But that's because we have fish!"
I said. "It would help if I had
an actual dog to draw."

"HA," said Stephen.
And, "HUH!" And, "You think
you can have a dog? Just because
you're special Nomi? When no one
in all these flats is allowed one?"
And, "HA! Get real, Nomi."

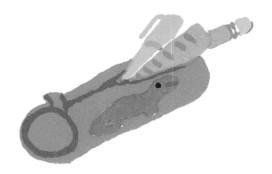

"HA," I said.
And, "HUH!"

And, "Think you can
be a dog do you,
Mallory? Just because
of your special
smile?"

And, **"HA, GET REAL, MALLORY!"**

And Mallory ... did!

"Mallory?" I said.

"Aruff!" said Mallory.

I wanted to tell everyone.

I didn't want anyone to know.

"What shall we do?" I said.

"Let's do everything."

We stuck our noses out to help us decide.
There was a leafy, rainy-tarmac smell.

"Aruff!" said Mallory.

"Good idea!" I said.

"Can I go outside?" I said.

"Well, Stephen's going
to the park," said Mum.
"Maybe he could take you along."

"But I'm going to play football," said
Stephen. "And I have to go now!"

"I'm ready," I said.

"What about breakfast?"
said Mum. "And shoes?"

"Breakfast," I said.
"And shoes."

At the park, Stephen found his football team.

We went to play,
but dogs are not
allowed in the
playground.

So I lent Mallory
my raincoat

and he tried not to
bark too much

(when he couldn't help it, I barked too).

Usually, I don't like it when Stephen
doesn't notice me. But Mallory and I
were too busy to think about that.

Then I wanted to go to the island.

So Mallory made an
arrangement with a coot.

We gave the birds our crisples

and then Brenda showed us
her favourite place to stand.

Then we all found treasure

and somewhere to live ...

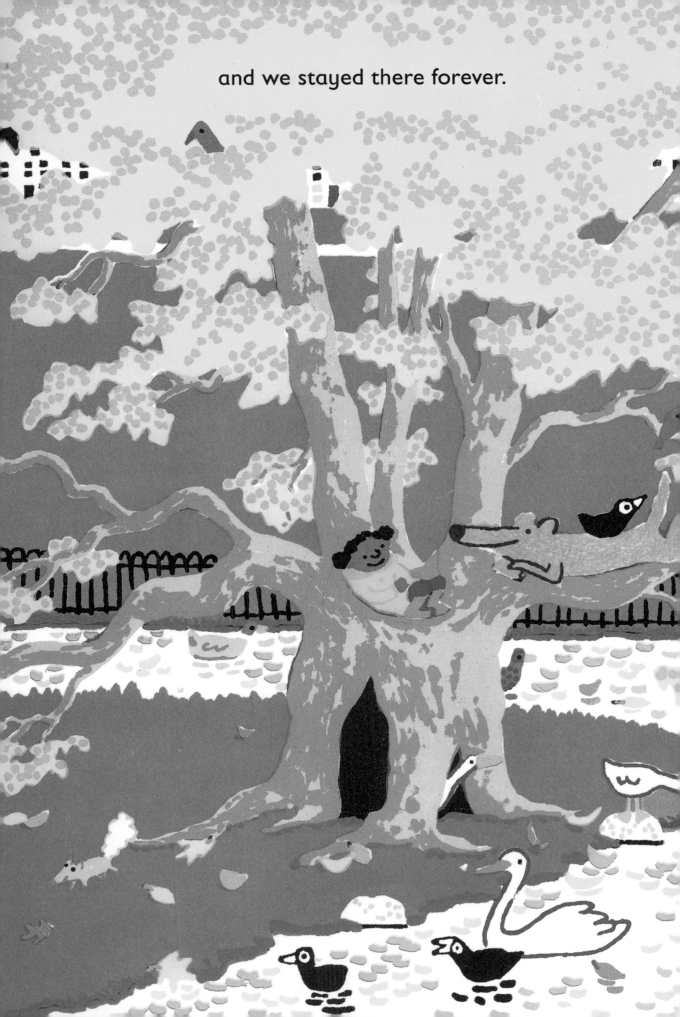

and we stayed there forever.

Until suddenly, I wished we still had the crisples.

"It can't always be breakfast time," I said.
(Mallory aruffed very softly.)

"Let's go and find Stephen," I said.

At home, Stephen told
us all about his brilliant,
incredible day. I said nothing.

After a while, Mum said,
"What about you, Nomi?"

I said nothing.

Stephen said, "Yeah, what
happened in Nomiland today?"

I said, "Well ... you know that dog
I drew? I told it to GET REAL, and
when I woke up, there was ...

Mallory?"

But I couldn't find
Mallory anywhere.

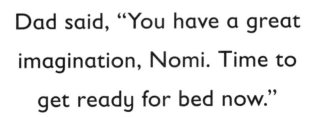

Dad said, "You have a great
imagination, Nomi. Time to
get ready for bed now."

I stared out at the darkness …

and there was Mallory, with stars around him.

"Mallory!" I said. "That's dangerous!
Come back here this instant."

"And next time, take me with you."

And after my story …

SUNRISE FOODS

Mallory did!

It all makes me think,
actually maybe I am quite
good at drawing dogs.